PEANUTS

Be a Good Sport, CHARLIE BROWN!

By Charles M. Schulz
Adapted by Jason Cooper
Illustrated by Vicki Scott

Simon Spotlight
New York   London   Toronto   Sydney   New Delhi

SIMON SPOTLIGHT
An imprint of Simon & Schuster Children's Publishing Division
1230 Avenue of the Americas, New York, New York 10020
This Simon Spotlight paperback edition January 2019
© 2019 Peanuts Worldwide LLC
All rights reserved, including the right of reproduction in whole or in part in any form.
SIMON SPOTLIGHT and colophon are registered trademarks of Simon & Schuster, Inc.
For information about special discounts for bulk purchases, please contact Simon & Schuster Special Sales
at 1-866-506-1949 or business@simonandschuster.com.
Manufactured in the United States of America 1218 LAK
2 4 6 8 10 9 7 5 3 1
ISBN 978-1-5344-3028-0
ISBN 978-1-5344-3029-7 (eBook)

Baseball season starts tomorrow and Charlie Brown can't wait. This year he is determined to do something he's never done before—win a game.

"I have high hopes for us this season," Charlie Brown says to his team. "As manager it's my job to make sure we focus, learn from past mistakes, and show everybody what we're made of!"

Lucy raises her hand. "Whose job is it to bring the snacks?" she asks.

"I've gathered the statistics from last season," Linus announces. "In twelve games we almost scored a run. In nine games we almost tagged a player out on first base. . . ."

The numbers are not impressive.

"In right field," Linus continues, "Lucy almost caught three pop flies." Charlie Brown sighs.

"Look at it this way, Charlie Brown," Linus reassures him. "We led the league in 'almosts'!"

"We're also the only team in the league with a beagle for a shortstop!" Schroeder says proudly.

Snoopy nods his head and thinks, *I heard a team a few years ago had a Labrador in left field, but he'd be retired by now.*

Charlie Brown and Linus walk home together after practice.
"That was a rousing speech you gave, Charlie Brown," Linus says. "Do you really think we can win this year?"

"We have the drive, and we have the determination!" Charlie Brown says.
"Yes, but do we have the talent?" Linus asks.
Charlie Brown thinks for a moment. "You know what they say," he admits.
"Two out of three's not bad. . . ."

That night Charlie Brown has trouble falling asleep. He always gets stressed when baseball season starts. "I worry about winning too much," he says to himself. "I need to remember that sports are supposed to be fun."

The next day Charlie Brown stands on the pitcher's mound. "Here we go," he says, "the very first pitch of the season!" He throws and *POW!* The ball flies past Charlie Brown, knocking him off the mound and blowing off his shoes and socks!

Charlie Brown lies on the ground, stunned. Lucy walks over.

"Did you catch the ball?" Charlie Brown asks.

"Of course not," Lucy says. "But I did pick it up when it stopped rolling."
Then Lucy looks at Charlie Brown's bare feet and giggles. "I had no idea your
toes were so cute!"

Charlie Brown is in no mood to accept a compliment. "Just get back to right
field!" he yells.

The game goes poorly, and the team loses.
"It's no fun losing 63–0!" Lucy says.
"At least it wasn't 64–0!" Charlie Brown reminds her.

"It's hard to tell if you're enthusiastic or delusional, but I appreciate your positivity!" Lucy tells Charlie Brown. Then she walks over to Schroeder and grabs his hand. "I also appreciate your catcher!"

"Good grief," groans Schroeder.

The team loses more games, and Charlie Brown starts to get frustrated. He knows it takes more than a good attitude to win. It also takes patience, practice, . . . and a shortstop who can stay awake during the game!

"Wake up, Snoopy!" Charlie Brown shouts.

Schroeder walks up to the pitcher's mound. "Do you think Beethoven would have liked me?" he asks Charlie Brown.

Charlie Brown grits his teeth. "Beethoven would have wanted you to focus on the game," he tells Schroeder.

"Interesting," Schroeder says. "I didn't know Beethoven even liked baseball."

"What's going on up there? Are you two talking about me?" Lucy yells from right field.

"*no!*" Charlie Brown yells back. "Concentrate on covering the outfield or we'll lose the game!"

Lucy shrugs. "Well, you learn more from losing than you do from winning."

Charlie Brown sighs. "That makes me the smartest person in the world. . . ."

The season is nearly over, and the team still hasn't won a game.
"We need ideas! How can we win tomorrow?" Charlie Brown asks.
"Pray for rain and hope the other team forfeits?" Pigpen suggests.
Lucy shakes her head. "I'd rather lose than win that way."
"Just what I need, a team full of good sports!" Charlie Brown yells.

Schroeder decides to leave practice early. "I'm going home to play piano. Beethoven is better than baseball."

"How is Beethoven better than baseball?!" Charlie Brown shouts.

"Because Beethoven would never yell at his team!" Schroeder declares.

The rest of the team agrees with Schroeder and leaves too.
Snoopy even sticks out his tongue at Charlie Brown as he walks past him.
"Why is everyone leaving? Don't you all want to win?" Charlie Brown asks.
"You said we would have fun, Charlie Brown," Lucy answers. "I've had more fun at the dentist!"

With his team gone, Charlie Brown stands all alone on the pitcher's mound.
"More fun at the dentist?" he says to himself. "That's terrible. . . ."
   Then it starts to rain. Charlie Brown looks at the clouds and cries, "You couldn't wait until tomorrow?"

The team was right. Charlie Brown had been so focused on winning that no one was having any fun. And baseball should be about having fun, not winning games!

That evening Charlie Brown calls each member of his team and apologizes for not being a good sport. He even gives Snoopy a special supper. "What do you say, pal? Friends again?"

Snoopy gives Charlie Brown a big hug and thinks, *Of course! Nothing says "I'm sorry" like dog treats!*

The following day Charlie Brown tells his team that for the rest of the season, they will focus on having fun.

"You don't care if we lose anymore?" Lucy asks.

"I suppose it would be nice to win, but it isn't everything," Charlie Brown replies. "Having fun with your friends is more important."

The team cheers, takes the field, and plays their best game of the year. In fact, they *almost* don't lose!

MEET CHARLIE BROWN'S TEAM!

Each baseball team has nine players with their own important position in the field:

- The **pitcher** throws the baseball to the other team's batter. Charlie Brown is the pitcher for the team . . . but he's not a very good one.

- The **catcher** guards home base. He works with the pitcher to prevent the other team from scoring a run. Schroeder is the catcher on Charlie Brown's team.

- The **first baseman** guards first base.

- The **second baseman** guards second base.

• The **third baseman** guards third base.

• The **shortstop** guards the area between second base and third base. Snoopy is a good shortstop . . . when he can stay awake!

• The **right fielder** is in charge of catching the ball in right field and throwing it back to the infield. Lucy plays right field on Charlie Brown's team.

• The **center fielder** and **left fielder** are responsible for catching the baseball in—you guessed it—center field and left field and throwing it back to the infield.

THE RULES OF BASEBALL

Every league has slightly different rules, but learning the basics of baseball will help you follow along in any baseball game!

Goal of the game

The goal of baseball is to score more points, or "runs," than the other team.

Baseball equipment

A **baseball** is a small round ball with stitching. You can't play baseball without a baseball!

The **bat** is a long, smooth stick that the batter uses to hit the baseball and score runs. Professional baseball players use bats made out of wood.

A **mitt** is a leather glove that helps a player catch the baseball. Each player wears a mitt while they are playing defense.

The structure of the game

The game is split up into innings. During an inning the teams each take a turn playing defense and offense. When a team plays offense, they try to score runs. The defensive team tries to stop the offensive team from scoring.

During a turn one of the batters from the offensive team stands at home base. When the defensive pitcher throws the ball, the batter swings. If the batter hits the ball, they run and tag first base. The defense tries to get the batter "out" by catching the ball before it hits the ground or tagging first base before the batter arrives.

If the batter makes it safely to first base, they must then make their way to second, third, and home base in order to score one run.

The turn ends when the defensive team gets three outs. Once both teams have taken their turn, the inning ends. At the end of nine innings, the team with more runs wins.

BE A GOOD SPORT!

No matter what sport or game you play, it's important to be a good sport. There are many different ways to show sportsmanship skills:

Play fair: Sometimes it's tempting to cheat in order to win. But remember that playing is about having fun, not winning—and it's not fun when people aren't playing by the rules!

Talk nicely. Don't trash-talk, which means saying insults to scare the other team. Respect umpires, referees, and other officials, too.

Support your teammates. If you're playing on a team, being a good sport means being a good teammate. Cheer on your teammates and compliment them on good plays. Make sure that everyone gets a chance to play, too.

Keep your cool. Even if the game isn't going well, try to stay calm. Charlie Brown couldn't keep his cool and yelled too much. But then he realized that yelling made everyone unhappy.

Be a good sport even after the game ends. If you lose, don't make excuses or blame other people for the loss. If you win, congratulations! But keep your celebration positive—don't brag or taunt the other players.

Play your best. No matter the score, you'll have fun and feel proud if you just try your best!

CHARLES SCHULZ LOVED SPORTS!

When Charles Schulz wasn't drawing the Peanuts comics, he enjoyed playing sports. In fact he based some of Charlie Brown's stories on his own sports experiences. Here are some facts you might not have known about Charles Schulz:

Charles Schulz played baseball as a kid. Once, his team lost a game 40–0 . . . but at least it wasn't 41–0!

Like Charlie Brown, Schulz was also the manager for his baseball team. Sometimes he played pitcher and sometimes he played catcher.

Schulz also liked playing ice hockey. He used to practice in his basement with tennis balls and a hockey stick. When he moved to Santa Rosa, California, Schulz built an ice rink two blocks away from his art studio. The rink was named Redwood Empire Ice Arena, but most people liked to call it Snoopy's Home Ice. Charles Schulz also played golf and tennis.

CHARLES SCHULZ'S WORDS OF WISDOM

Charles Schulz had many words of wisdom about being a good sport:

"A game between two teams in 7th and 10th place can be just as exciting as any game. But all we're worrying about is who wins. It should be the plays, great goals being scored, great baskets being made, great overhand shots hit. These are the things that count in sports."

"Defeat is a lot funnier than victory. Most of us know what it is like to lose some kind of contest, and we can identify with that. How wonderful it must be, thousands of people admire the person who is holding up the trophy. But we forget also that somebody had to lose and we can all identify much more closely with losing than winning because most of us have lost."

Play ball!